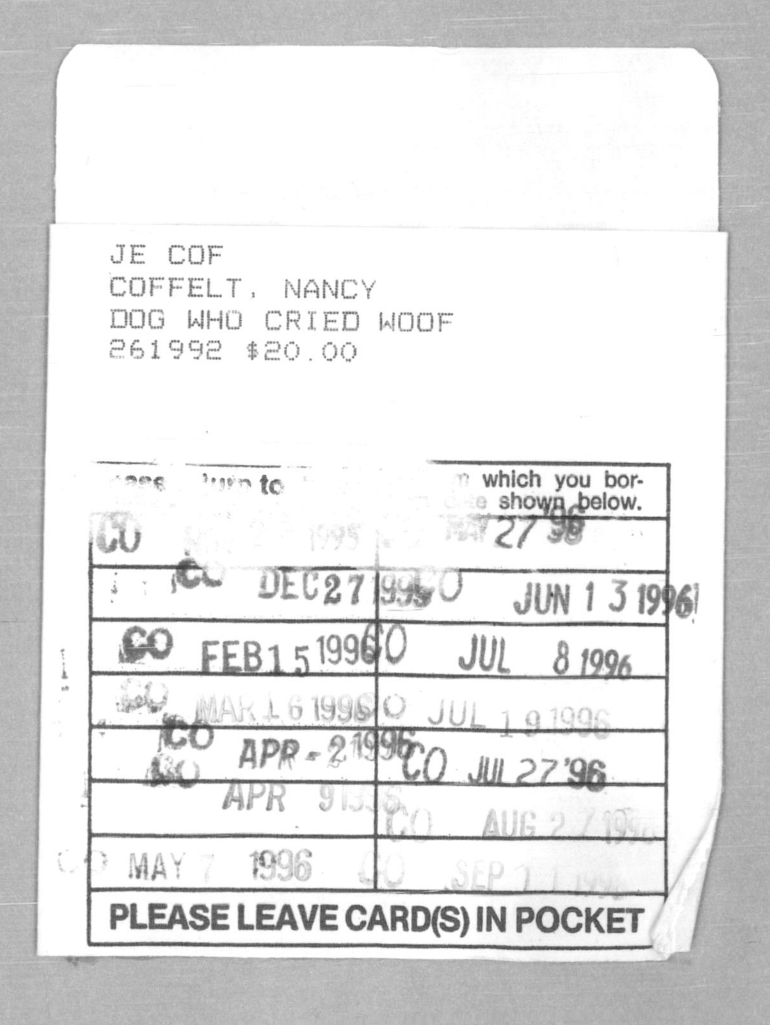

THE DOG WHO CRIED WOOF

NANCY COFFELT

GULLIVER BOOKS
HARCOURT BRACE & COMPANY
SAN DIEGO NEW YORK LONDON

Library of Congress Cataloging-in-Publication Data
Coffelt, Nancy.
The dog who cried woof/Nancy Coffelt.—1st ed.
p. cm.
"Gulliver books."
Summary: Ernie the dog barks so much that when he tries to warn people about a sneaky orange cat stealing his food, nobody pays any attention.
ISBN 0-15-200201-4
[1. Dogs—Fiction. 2. Cats—Fiction. 3. Noise—Fiction 4. Barking—Fiction.] I. Title.
PZ7.C658Dm 1995
[E]—dc20 94-5653

First edition A B C D E

Printed in Singapore

The illustrations in this book were done in Caran D'ache oil pastels on black Canson paper.
The display type was set in Bovine Poster.
The text type was set in Memphis Medium by Harcourt Brace & Company Photocomposition Center, San Diego, California.
Color separations by Bright Arts, Ltd., Hong Kong
Printed and bound by Tien Wah Press, Singapore
This book was printed with soya-based inks on Leykam recycled paper, which contains more than 20 percent postconsumer waste and has a total recycled content of at least 50 percent.
Production supervision by Warren Wallerstein and David Hough
Designed by Camilla Filancia

For my friend Joe Durrett,
who loved his own barker, Magnolia

Ernie was a dog. He was a huge and very hairy dog. Ernie was actually quite a nice dog. But, most of all, Ernie was a *loud* dog.

Ernie barked at everything that moved and at many things that didn't. If a bird flew into the yard, Ernie barked. If a squirrel climbed the big tree across the street, Ernie barked.

If a leaf fell, a flower bloomed, or the wind changed direction, Ernie barked and barked and barked some more.

The people in the house tried to get Ernie to be quiet. "No!" they would say, or "Shhh!"

Sometimes that helped. But not for long. There was always something new for Ernie to bark at.

When the people got sick of listening to Ernie, they walked around the house with their hands over their ears. But their arms got tired.

Finally they bought earmuffs. When they wore them, Ernie's loud barks faded to dull woofs.

One summer day new people moved in next door and brought a big orange cat with them. That big orange cat was trouble!

It lurked in the garden. Ernie barked. It slithered through the hedges. Ernie barked.

The big orange cat even slipped into Ernie's house through the kitchen window. Ernie barked and jumped up and down.

But the cat simply ignored him and stole hot dog buns from the counter. Ernie barked until his hair stood on end. The big orange cat just flicked its tail.

Then, one day, the slinky orange cat ate Ernie's own dog food out of Ernie's own dish. The people in the house didn't see the cat. But Ernie did.

Ernie desperately tried to tell the people. He barked loud, louder, and even louder barks. But the people were fed up with Ernie's noise. "Be quiet!" they shouted, and readjusted their earmuffs.

Day after day Ernie barked as he watched the big orange cat steal his food.

Ernie's throat became so tired from all that barking that he finally lost his voice.

When all the barking stopped, something amazing happened. The people took off their earmuffs. They didn't say "No!" and "Shhh!"

Instead they said things like "Good dog!" and "Want a biscuit?" Ernie liked the attention and the biscuits. But he missed his bark.

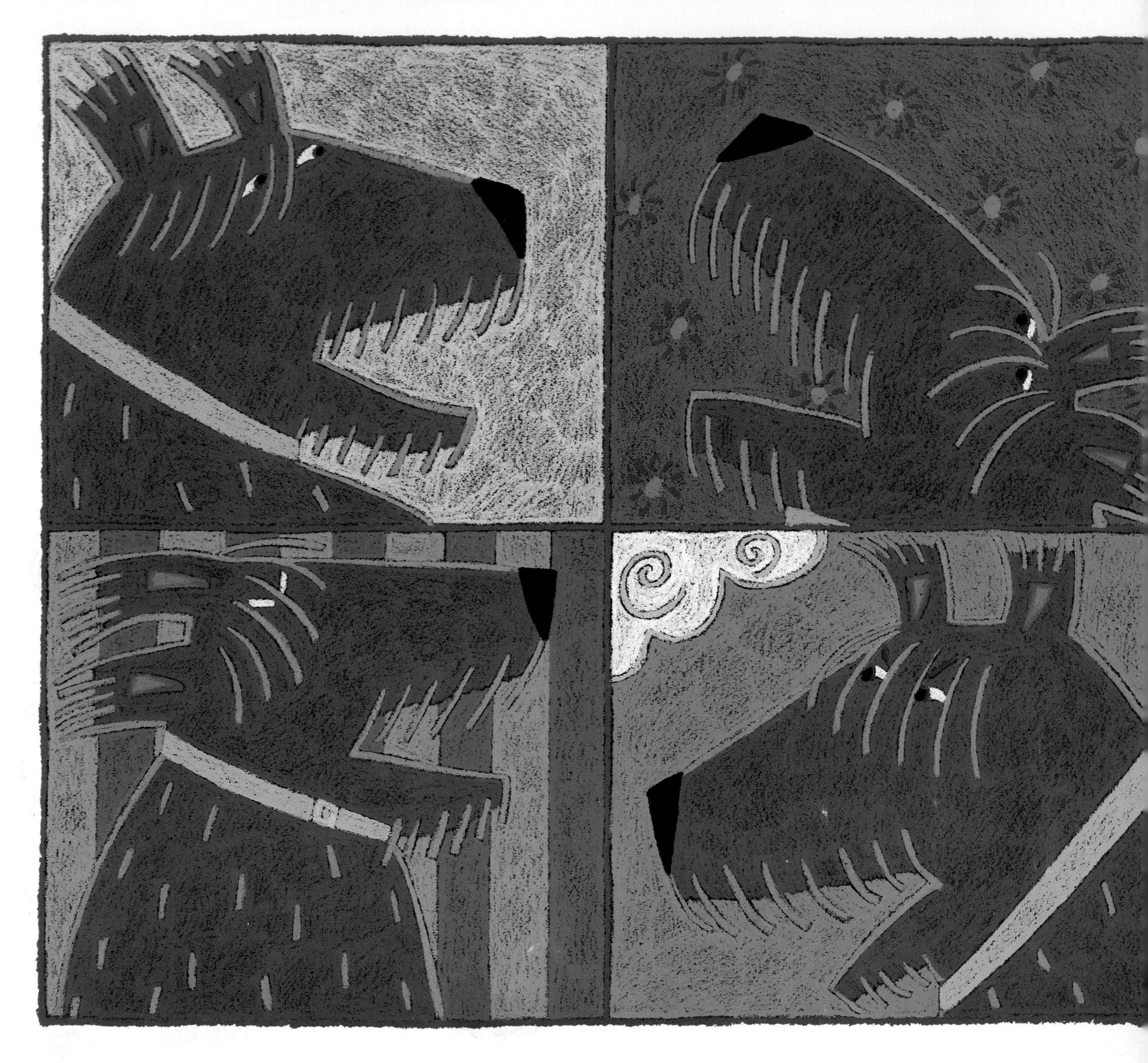

Each day for seven long days Ernie tried to bark. Nothing happened. Then, on the eighth morning, he managed a whine.

Ernie was thrilled. His voice was back!

He rumbled a growl at the squirrel and even gave a few quiet woofs to tell the people the mail had arrived. But Ernie saved his really loud barks.

Somehow a leaf falling or a flower blooming didn't seem nearly as important when Ernie still had a problem like the cat to worry about.

Ernie was taking a nap when the big orange cat snuck through the kitchen, narrowed its eyes, and headed straight for the dog dish.

Ernie jumped up and exploded into a fury of barking. His barks filled the kitchen. The cat, who hadn't heard Ernie bark for a week, stopped eating in midchew.

Ernie's barks were louder than ever before. They flowed out of the kitchen and up the stairs.

The people, who also hadn't heard Ernie bark in days, came running to see what all the commotion was about.

They arrived just in time to see the slinky orange cat committing its terrible crime. "Good boy!" the people told Ernie.

"Bad cat!" they said as they dumped the horrible, sneaky cat out the very same window it had come in.

The next day the people put in a screen. Now the cat only looks at Ernie's food, and the people only wear their earmuffs in winter. Ernie usually saves his barks for important events, like when the mail arrives or the doorbell rings. But once in a while Ernie barks at the wind, just because he wants to.